NORTH AMERICAN DINOSAURS

TRICERATOPS

ANASTASIA SUEN

ROurke
Educational Media

A Division of
Carson Dellosa
Education

rourkeeducationalmedia.com

Before Reading: *Building Background Knowledge and Vocabulary*

Building background knowledge can help children process new information and build upon what they already know. Before reading a book, it is important to tap into what children already know about the topic. This will help them develop their vocabulary and increase their reading comprehension.

Questions and Activities to Build Background Knowledge:

1. Look at the front cover of the book and read the title. What do you think this book will be about?
2. What do you already know about this topic?
3. Take a book walk and skim the pages. Look at the table of contents, photographs, captions, and bold words. Did these text features give you any information or predictions about what you will read in this book?

Vocabulary: *Vocabulary Is Key to Reading Comprehension*

Use the following directions to prompt a conversation about each word.

- Read the vocabulary words.
- What comes to mind when you see each word?
- What do you think each word means?

> ### Vocabulary Words:
> - *carnivores*
> - *coprolite*
> - *cycads*
> - *dung*
> - *frill*
> - *herbivore*
> - *herd*
> - *paleontologist*
> - *plesiosaurs*
> - *territory*

During Reading: *Reading for Meaning and Understanding*

To achieve deep comprehension of a book, children are encouraged to use close reading strategies. During reading, it is important to have children stop and make connections. These connections result in deeper analysis and understanding of a book.

 Close Reading a Text

During reading, have children stop and talk about the following:

- Any confusing parts
- Any unknown words
- Text to text, text to self, text to world connections
- The main idea in each chapter or heading

Encourage children to use context clues to determine the meaning of any unknown words. These strategies will help children learn to analyze the text more thoroughly as they read.

When you are finished reading this book, turn to the next-to-last page for **Text-Dependent Questions** and an **Extension Activity**.

TABLE OF CONTENTS

The Bone Wars 4

Coprolite Clues 11

Horns and Frills 16

A Herd 20

Extinct! 24

Time Line: *Triceratops* and You 29

Glossary 30

Index 31

Text-Dependent Questions 31

Extension Activity 31

About the Author 32

THE BONE WARS

Othniel Charles Marsh collected fossils. He found the remains of plants and animals from long ago. Marsh was a **paleontologist**. So was his friend, Edward Drinker Cope. But their friendship turned into a big fight. It was called the Bone Wars. Both men wanted to name the most fossils.

Cope went out to dig for fossils every year. But his old friend Marsh only did that four times. After that, he stayed at Yale University. He was a professor there. Professor Marsh sent others out to do the digging for him.

Edward Drinker Cope

Othniel Charles Marsh was a professor at Yale University in New Haven, Connecticut.

CANADA

Lake Manitoba

Lake of
the Woods

Lake
Nipigon

Missouri

MONTANA

NORTH DAKOTA

Red Lake

MINNESOTA

Lake Superior

WISCONSIN

Mississippi

Lake Michigan

MICHIG

WYOMING

SOUTH DAKOTA

Missouri

IOWA

ILLINOIS

INDIANA

UTAH

Green

Colorado

COLORADO

NEBRASKA

Arkansas

KANSAS

MISSOURI

KENTUCKY

Rocky Mountains

NEW
MEXICO

Rio Grande

Arkansas

OKLAHOMA

Red

ARKANSAS

Arkansas

TENNESSEE

Tennessee

Red

TEXAS

Red

Mississippi

MISSISSIPPI

ALABAMA

Rio Grande

LOUISIANA

MEXICO

GULF OF MEXICO

One of the people who dug up fossils for Professor Marsh was John Bell Hatcher. He lived in Iowa as a boy. To pay for college, Hatcher worked in a coal mine. Deep in the mine, he found fossils, too. Hatcher started collecting them.

Hatcher met Professor Marsh at Yale. After graduating in 1884, he started collecting fossils for the professor. Hatcher started in Kansas. Then he looked for fossils in Texas, Nebraska, South Dakota, and Wyoming.

The King of Collectors

Hatcher sent the fossils he collected back to Yale. He discovered that anthills were a good place to dig. The ants dug up small bones as they made their homes. They moved the bones up to the top. Hatcher found many small mammal bones on top of anthills. In October and November of 1888, he sent 71 boxes of fossils. They weighed 15,410 pounds (6,990 kilograms). Professor Marsh called Hatcher the "King of Collectors."

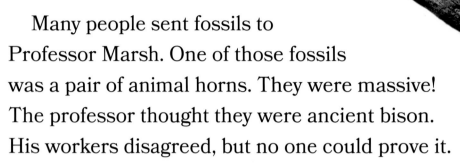

Many people sent fossils to Professor Marsh. One of those fossils was a pair of animal horns. They were massive! The professor thought they were ancient bison. His workers disagreed, but no one could prove it.

In 1889, the professor sent Hatcher to Wyoming. There, he dug up the skull of an animal with massive horns. He sent it to Yale. It matched the other horns.

The professor changed his mind. The massive horns weren't from a bison. They were from a dinosaur. He named it *Triceratops horridus*. *Triceratops* means "three-horned face." *Horridus* is Latin for "terrifying."

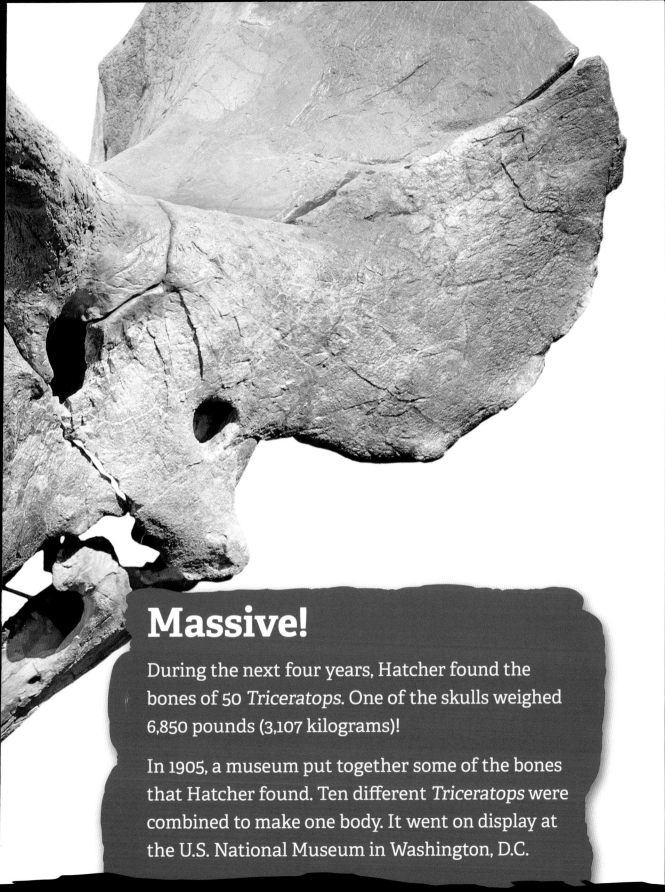

Massive!

During the next four years, Hatcher found the bones of 50 *Triceratops*. One of the skulls weighed 6,850 pounds (3,107 kilograms)!

In 1905, a museum put together some of the bones that Hatcher found. Ten different *Triceratops* were combined to make one body. It went on display at the U.S. National Museum in Washington, D.C.

COPROLITE CLUES

Scientists know about dinosaurs because of clues they left behind. They left behind bones. They left behind eggs and **dung**. They left behind tracks in the mud.

Sometimes these remains hardened over time into rocks. Rock bones, eggs, tracks, and dung are called fossils. Yes, dinosaur poop turned into fossils! The fancy name for fossilized dinosaur dung is **coprolite**.

The fossilized dung shows what *Triceratops* ate. When *Triceratops* roamed the land, it was not covered with grass. It was covered with ferns, **cycads**, palm trees, and flowering shrubs. The clues in the coprolite tell scientists that *Triceratops* was an **herbivore**. It only ate plants.

Triceratops had huge, powerful jaws. With its beak like a parrot's, it slashed through branches. It snapped tough fern stalks. Then its sharp back teeth cut the greens like scissors. New teeth were constantly growing in. Some adult dinosaurs had three rows of teeth on both sides!

Stomping after *Triceratops* was *Tyrannosaurus rex*. *T. rex* was king. This dinosaur was the biggest of the Rocky Mountain meat eaters, or **carnivores**. *T. rex* could attack an injured or sick *Triceratops*. It could catch a baby *Triceratops*, or an old one. Parts of *Triceratops* have been found in the fossilized dung of *T. rex*.

In 1998, the very first *Triceratops* skeleton was taken down. The workers at the museum took it apart. They made casts of the bones.

Now that more bones had been discovered, the scientists knew more. They made some of the bone casts bigger. They made others smaller. The new skeleton was named Hatcher, after John.

By this time, the museum had a new name too. Now it was called the Smithsonian Museum of Natural History.

In 2019, Hatcher was built all over again. This time he was lying on the ground under a *T. rex*!

HORNS AND FRILLS

Triceratops could use its horns to push down trees and chomp the tops. When attacked, *Triceratops* thrust and charged with its horns. When *T. rex* came too near, a whole *Triceratops* **herd** may have charged. Or they may have grouped up and faced their horns out. Together, they'd be like a giant porcupine. *T. rex* would have to get dinner someplace else.

Triceratops didn't use its horns much for jousting with *T. rex*, though. It mostly used its horns for fighting off other *Triceratops*. These animals clacked and locked horns, like deer and elk do. They probably fought over mates or **territory**.

The head of a *Triceratops* was almost one-third the size of its entire body. The bony fan at the back was the **frill**. It wasn't as hard as armor. Some *Triceratops* skulls have holes pierced in the frills.

The skin of *Triceratops* was bumpy and rough. The frill was probably brightly colored. These colors could attract a mate. The bigger the head and the brighter the frill, the easier it was to meet a mate.

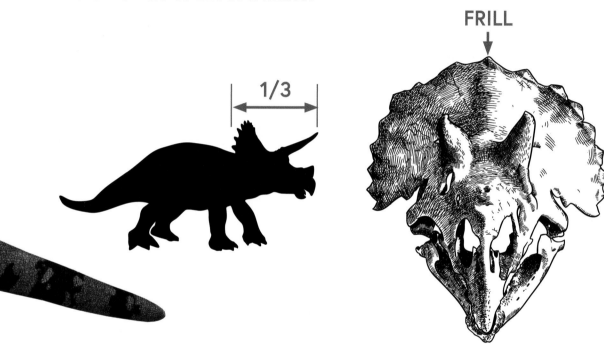

FRILL

1/3

Chill Your Frill

Warm-blooded animals tend to have more blood vessels than cold-blooded animals. Scientists find many signs of a large amount of blood vessels on *Triceratops* skulls.

Triceratops may have used the blood vessels in its frill to cool off. That is how modern elephants use their ears to cool off.

A HERD

The tracks of *Triceratops* show it moved in herds like elephants do. It walked slowly, but it could probably run up to about 25 miles (40 kilometers) an hour. It probably protected its young by keeping them in the middle of the herd.

Triceratops walked on all fours. Its footprint was about 20 inches (51 centimeters) wide. Each front foot had five flat toes. The two back feet had four flat toes each.

It could rear up on its back legs like an elephant. It may have slept like a horse. Horses lock their knees to sleep standing up.

Some dinosaur eggs have been found in nests. For this reason, scientists think that *Triceratops* laid its eggs in nests. The adults might have watched over the eggs.

After *Triceratops* hatched, it may have been ready to eat palms. At some point, a hatchling could eat on its own and join the herd.

Growth Rings

The bones of dinosaurs have growth rings inside. Scientists count the rings. This tells them the age of the dinosaurs when they died. Scientists use computers to compare the bones and tracks of dinosaurs to the muscles, bones, and tracks of animals alive now.

EXTINCT!

At one time, *Triceratops* was among the most numerous of the dinosaurs. Yet it died out. It was among the last dinosaurs to become extinct.

Triceratops lived long, long ago near the Rocky Mountains. It was so long ago that no person was there to see them. The Rocky Mountains were very young. The mountains edged a saltwater sea. *Triceratops* ambled over the nearby hot, wet plains.

CRETACEOUS SEA LIFE

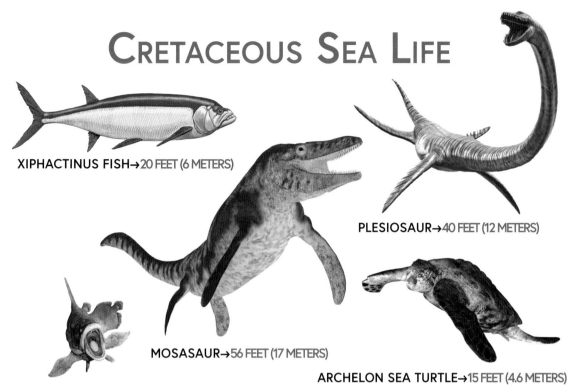

XIPHACTINUS FISH→20 FEET (6 METERS)

PLESIOSAUR→40 FEET (12 METERS)

MOSASAUR→56 FEET (17 METERS)

ARCHELON SEA TURTLE→15 FEET (4.6 METERS)

MAWSONIA FISH→6.5 FEET (2 METERS)

SAURODON FISH→8.5 FEET (2.6 METERS)

CRETOXYRHINA SHARK→26 FEET (8 METERS)

PLATYPTERYGIUS→23 FEET (7 METERS)

By the Saltwater Sea

While *Triceratops* wandered the plains, other dinosaurs rambled through the woods. Turtles, frogs, and crocodiles slid into the waters. Fish and **plesiosaurs** swam there too. Small mammals scurried around on the shores. But there were no wolves, cougars, or bears.

Why did all of the *Triceratops* die? Some experts believe that the seasons grew too cold and icy. Other experts think that volcanoes erupted, or a gigantic boulder from space hit Earth. The skies might have turned black. The air would have been poisoned and the sunlight blocked. Plants probably died. Then dinosaurs that ate plants died. And the dinosaurs that ate other dinosaurs died.

No one knows exactly what happened. Scientists are still looking for clues. But they do know that *Triceratops* was one of the heaviest and toughest plant-eating dinosaurs ever.

Alberta

Saskatchewan

Montana

North Dakota

Wyoming

South Dakota

Colorado

Where to Hunt Dinosaurs

Triceratops fossils have all been found near the Rocky Mountains. This mountain range is in the western United States and Canada. In Canada, they were found in Alberta and Saskatchewan. In the United States, these fossils have been dug up in Wyoming, Montana, Colorado, North Dakota, and South Dakota. *Triceratops* is the state fossil of South Dakota.

Time Line:
Triceratops and You

Do you see yourself on the time line? Look at the far right. You live in the Quaternary Period of the Cenozoic Era. Dinosaurs lived in the era before ours. They roamed Earth in the Mesozoic Era.

The Mesozoic Era had three time periods. *Triceratops* lived in the last one. They were Cretaceous dinosaurs. They lived on Earth 68 to 66 million years ago.

Triceratops
68–66 million years ago

YOU!

MESOZOIC			CENOZOIC	
Triassic 251–199.6 million years ago	**Jurassic** 199.6–145.5 million years ago	**Cretaceous** 145.5–65.5 million years ago	**Tertiary** 65.5–1.81 million years ago	**Quaternary** 1.81–NOW million years ago

GLOSSARY

carnivores (KAHR-nuh-vors): animals that eat other animals

coprolite (KAH-pruh-lite): a fossil rock of animal poop

cycads (SYE-kuhds): large, hot-weather plants with leaves like a palm or fern

dung (duhng): animal poop

frill (fril): a large wavy collar around the neck

herbivore (HUR-buh-vor): an animal that eats only plants

herd (hurd): a group of animals that live and move together

paleontologist (pay-lee-ahn-TAH-luh-jist): a person who studies ancient life

plesiosaurs (PLEE-see-uh-sors): reptiles with long necks that swam in the water during the Jurassic and Cretaceous periods

territory (TER-i-tor-ee): land

INDEX

bone(s) 4, 7, 9, 11, 14, 23

Cope, Edward Drinker 4

eggs 11, 23

fossil(s) 4, 7, 8, 11, 28

Hatcher, John Bell 7

horns 8, 16

Marsh, Othniel Charles 4, 5

museum 9, 14

Rocky Mountain(s) 13, 24, 28

Tyrannosaurus rex 13

TEXT-DEPENDENT QUESTIONS

1. How were fossils found for the Bone Wars?

2. Why do you think the museum gave their *Triceratops* a new name in 1998?

3. Describe a *Triceratops* head.

4. How do growth rings help scientists?

5. What other animals were alive when *Triceratops* was?

EXTENSION ACTIVITY

Practice your paleontology skills! Many museums have models of dinosaur bones in rocks. Use air-dry clay to make a model of a *Triceratops* fossil in a rock. Allow two days for the model to dry. Place a few drops of brown tempera paint on the clay and rub it with a sponge. Then rub the clay with a paper towel to remove any extra paint. If desired, add a coat of black or tan paint.

ABOUT THE AUTHOR

Anastasia Suen is the author of more than 300 books for young readers. Her children were both dinosaur fans, so she took them to the Natural History Museum of Los Angeles County and the La Brea Tar Pits often. They called both of these sites the "dinosaur" museum!

© 2020 Rourke Educational Media

www.rourkeeducationalmedia.com

PHOTO CREDITS: Cover and Title Page ©Joe Tucciarone ; Pg 4 ©Frederick Gutekunst @ Wiki; Pg 5 ©Wiki; Pg 5 ©f11photo; Pg 6 ©Bardocz Peter ; Pg 7 ©Wiki; Pg 8 ©herraez; Pg 10 ©powerofforever; Pg 11 ©novielysa; Pg 12 ©Herschel Hoffmeyer; Pg 14 ©RiverNorthPhotography; Pg 15 ©François Gohier; Pg 16, 25 ©CoreyFord; Pg 17 ©para827; Pg 18 ©Vac1; Pg 19 ©Andrii-Oliinyk; Pg 20 ©dottedhippo; Pg 20 ©para827; Pg 22 ©Hall Train Studios; Pg 23 ©somethingway; Pg 24 ©Orla; Pg 25 ©Warpaintcobra, Damouraptor @ Wiki, Dmitry Bogdanov @ Wiki, Vac1, Bogdanov dmitrchel @ Wiki, DiBgd @ Wiki; Pg 26 ©Jagoush, Zloyel, Andrew_Mayovskyy; Pg 18, 28, 29 ©oktaydegirmenci; Pg 29 ©ChrisGorgio

Edited by: Kim Thompson
Cover design by: Rhea Magaro-Wallace
Interior design by: Janine Fisher

Library of Congress PCN Data

Triceratops / Anastasia Suen
(North American Dinosaurs)
ISBN 978-1-73161-450-6 (hard cover)
ISBN 978-1-73161-245-8 (soft cover)
ISBN 978-1-73161-555-8 (e-Book)
ISBN 978-1-73161-660-9 (ePub)
Library of Congress Control Number: 2019932150

Rourke Educational Media
Printed in the United States of America,
North Mankato, Minnesota